LOONIVERSE
STRANGER THINGS

BY **DAVID LUBAR**

ILLUSTRATED BY
MATT LOVERIDGE

BRANCHES
SCHOLASTIC INC.

Read all the

LOONIVERSE books!

#1

#2

#3

#4

table of contents

FOR JOELLE AND ALISON—DL

Library of Congress Cataloging-in-Publication Data
Lubar, David.
Stranger things / by David Lubar ; illustrated by Matt Loveridge. p. cm. — (Looniverse ; #1)
Summary: When ordinary third-grader Ed finds a coin with the words "strange" and "stranger" on both sides, weird things start happening around him—but when his friends start blaming him for all the weirdness Ed wonders if this coin is not too strange for comfort.
ISBN 978-0-545-49602-5 (pbk. : alk. paper)
ISBN 978-0-545-49601-8 (reinforced hardcover library binding : alk. paper)
ISBN 978-0-545-49685-8 (ebook)
1. Coins—Juvenile fiction. 2. Magic—Juvenile fiction. 3. Friendship—Juvenile fiction. [1. Coins—Fiction.
2. Magic—Fiction. 3. Friendship—Fiction.] I. Loveridge, Matt, ill. II. Title.
PZ7.L96775St 2013
813.54--dc23
2012024838

ISBN 978-0-545-49601-8 (hardcover) / ISBN 978-0-545-49602-5 (paperback)

12 11 10 9 8 7 6 5 4 3 2   13 14 15 16 17 18/0

Printed in China   38
First Scholastic printing, May 2013

Illustrated by Matt Loveridge
Book design by Liz Herzog

chapter 1

A SILVER SURPRISE

I was walking home from school on a Friday afternoon when I stumbled across the coin. And I do mean *stumbled.* Right after I crossed Ridge Street, I tripped on the curb and fell. Luckily, I landed on a soft strip of grass. A silvery circle flashed and glittered beneath my nose.

I stared down at a large coin. As soon as I touched it, the strangest thing happened. The moon rose like a hard-smacked, high fly ball. It set just as quickly, dropping out of a bright blue sky.

"No way," I said.

Maybe I'd fallen harder than I thought. The coin felt icy cold, even though the air was warm. The same two words were on each side of it: **STRANGE, STRANGER.**

That sure wasn't the sort of coin anyone would ever give to me. I'm as far from strange as possible. Everyone else has talents, hobbies, or adventures worth talking about. Not me. I'm just plain old normal Ed, a third grader at Complex Elementary School.

I started to get up, but then froze. A man was shuffling along the sidewalk in the oddest way. After every couple steps, he dropped to his knees, moving his head like a hunting dog and running his hands through the grass.

Step, drop, search, stand.

Step, drop, search, stand.

It was almost like a dance.

When the man got closer, I recognized him. It was Mr. Sage, the owner of the New Curiosity Shop. My mom goes there when she needs a present for someone who has everything. I thought "curiosity" meant you wanted to know something. But Mom said that a curiosity can also be an interesting object. That shop sure has plenty of those!

When Mr. Sage reached me, he dropped to his knees and ran one hand through the grass right next to my face. His sleeve smelled like old books.

I wrapped my fingers around the coin. "Did you lose something?" I asked.

"No. I'm trying to find something," he said. He didn't seem surprised that I was lying there.

"What are you trying to find?" I asked, hoping it wasn't a coin.

He laughed. "I won't know until I find it."

"Good luck." I realized I'd been squeezing the coin real hard.

"Thank you." He stood and walked past me, then continued his weird step-drop-search-stand routine. *Maybe being normal isn't so bad,* I thought as I got up.

I headed down the block to meet my little brother, Derwin. He goes to kindergarten at Albert Camus Primary School. He was just coming out the door when I got there.

Derwin

When Derwin spotted me, he jumped like he'd been startled. "Amazing! What a great idea!" he shouted. Then he raced right past me like he was riding a rocket.

I stuck the coin in my pocket and headed home. *What was Derwin so excited about?* I wondered.

chapter 2

A NUMBER OF WORDS

I found Derwin in the living room, working hard at something. I could tell that he was working hard, because his mouth was open and his tongue was hanging out. It made his face look sort of like an untied shoe.

"What are you writing?" I asked him.

"Words," he said, not looking up. He barely seemed to notice I was there.

I glanced at the papers spread out around him. They were filled with rows of words.

"That's a lot of words," I said.

"It has to be," Derwin said. He stopped to sharpen his pencil.

I read one of the pages:

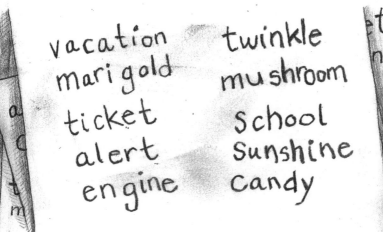

vacation   twinkle
marigold   mushroom
ticket   school
alert   sunshine
engine   candy

I waited for Derwin to explain what he was doing, but he just kept writing. I went to the kitchen table and did my homework. After that, I fed my pets. By then, it was almost dinnertime. When I came back into the living room, Derwin was still working. "Nine hundred ninety-eight," he said as he wrote.

"Nine hundred ninety-nine. One thousand!" He gathered up all of the papers and dashed out the door.

Okay, this was getting stranger. I couldn't resist following him any more than I could resist a chocolate fudge brownie.

Derwin raced down the street and around the corner. He ran up to a small yellow house and knocked on the door. I stayed nearby, waiting to see what would happen next.

A tall, thin man stepped onto the porch. Derwin handed him the papers. The man studied each sheet. Then he held up his index finger and said, "Very good. Wait here."

The man went inside. A moment later, he returned and gave something to Derwin.

"Thank you," Derwin said. He stepped off the porch and headed toward me.

The curiosity was killing me. "What is it?" I asked when Derwin reached the sidewalk.

"A picture," he said. He held up a fabulous painting of a dragon.

"It's wonderful. But why'd he give it to you?" I asked.

"I gave him a thousand words," Derwin said. "Last week, you told me **'A PICTURE IS WORTH A THOUSAND WORDS'** when you were explaining the difference between African and Asian elephants. Remember?"

I remembered telling him that when I'd found the photos online. Until now though, I'd assumed it was just a saying. It looked like Derwin had made it become real.

I'd love to get my own amazing picture. I thought about bringing a thousand words to the man in the yellow house. But I knew it would be a waste of time. I wouldn't get a picture. Or if I did, it would be a picture of a mud puddle, a broken egg, or something else I didn't want.

That's just how things seem to work for me. Sure, I'd found a coin, but it wasn't all that special.

Derwin walked off, humming.

I watched him go. He'd always been strange, but he'd never done anything this strange. Then, at dinner, things got a whole lot stranger. . . .

MEAL ON WHEELS

My older sister, Sarah Beth, loves art. She's always drawing, painting, and sculpting. She even makes things out of food. Last week, at dinner, she built a model of the Eiffel Tower using carrot sticks. Our parents don't stop her, because they like to encourage creativity.

Sarah Beth creates her biggest projects on the holidays, when there's lots of food on the table. Tonight wasn't a holiday, but we had tons of food. We were having what my parents call "Practice-Giving" dinner. They get so worried that everything won't be perfect on Thanksgiving, when all the relatives come here, that they make practice dinners in September and October. That's strange, but fine with me. I love turkey and gravy. Besides, parents are supposed to be strange.

Even though there was room at the big table, Sarah Beth, Derwin, my little sister Libby, and I sat at the kids' table. That's part of the practice. As soon as we took our seats, Sarah Beth grabbed some slices of cranberry sauce and leaned them against a stack of turkey. She tied the whole thing up with string beans.

"What are you making?" I asked as I helped myself to mashed potatoes and a drumstick.

"Guess," she said, giving me a big grin.

"Is it a truck?" I asked.

"Nope—it's not a truck." Sarah Beth stuck an olive on the turkey part, near the front. Then she balanced another olive on top of it.

I glanced at my parents. They were so used to Sarah Beth making things that they didn't seem to notice what she was doing. Derwin and Libby weren't paying attention to her, either. My dog, Rex, and my cat, Willow, paid attention, hoping something tasty would fall to the floor.

Rex

Willow

"Is it a bus?" I guessed as I drowned my potatoes in gravy.

"You're getting warm," she said. She grabbed the pitcher from me and poured gravy into the tower of olives.

I took another guess. "A subway car?"

"You're warmer," she said. "Guess again."

I watched the steam from the gravy rise out of the olives "A train!" I said, suddenly realizing that the olives were a smoke stack.

"Yup," Sarah Beth said. "It's a chew chew train," she joked.

The train rolled off her plate. "Whoa!" I gasped as it chugged across the table, right toward me!

chapter 4

DANGEROUS STORIES

I sat there, too amazed to move, as the train pushed my plate onto my lap.

"Wow — I guess it turned out to be a steam train," Sarah Beth said.

"No kidding," I said as the steaming hot gravy dripped on my shoes, and my drumstick rolled off the plate. She'd really meant it when she'd said I was getting warmer.

Rex grabbed the drumstick and ran off. Willow batted a string bean across the floor.

"Ed, stop playing with your food," Dad said.

"And clean up that mess," Mom said.

"Me? But . . ." I pointed at Sarah Beth, but I realized there was nothing I could say. My parents hadn't seen the train chug across the table.

Maybe I hadn't, either. Maybe Sarah Beth had tipped the table. Really, that was the only explanation that made sense.

There was no way the train could have moved by itself. Either way, it had made a big mess. Sarah Beth helped me clean up.

That night, Libby brought me a picture book. "Read to me," she said.

Libby has a wild imagination. If I read a story to her about crocodiles, she'll spend the next day telling me there's a crocodile hiding under the couch. So I have to keep peeking under the couch to prove to her that everything is okay.

Libby

"Not tonight," I told her. "I've had a strange day, and a lap full of food."

"Please," she said. "I love the way you do all the voices."

I looked at the title of the book. *The Pied Piper.* That seemed fairly harmless — no scary creatures. "Okay," I said.

Libby curled up next to me, and I read her the story. It's about a musician who lures the rats out of the town of Hamelin by playing his flute.

By the time I was finished, she was fast asleep. She was lucky. Even if I hadn't had this whole day full of strange experiences to think about, I was too excited to fall asleep. My best friend, Moose, was having a pool party tomorrow for his birthday. It was going to be at the big hotel in town, and it was going to be awesome.

I hope tomorrow isn't as strange as today, I thought as I drifted off.

It turned out to be much stranger.

chapter 5

MICE TO MEET YOU

Saturday morning, Libby marched across the living room. She was blowing into a soda straw and making flute sounds. As I put my hand in my pocket and felt the coin, I thought about how both Derwin and Sarah Beth had suddenly gotten a whole lot stranger.

Not you, too, I thought.

Yes. Her, too. She had five mice at her heels. *At least they aren't rats,* I thought. As Libby marched in circles around the living room, the crowd of rodents grew larger and larger.

I wasn't afraid of mice, but I wasn't happy being around so many of them — especially when more and more kept coming.

"Libby," I said as the mice began to form a second layer, "that's enough."

She didn't hear me over the squeaking. One mouse doesn't make much noise, but when you fill a room with mice, the squeaks become a roar.

"LIBBY!" I shouted. "THAT'S ENOUGH!"

She took the straw from her lips. "Enough?"

"Yeah. The mice can't stay," I said.

"Why not?" Libby asked.

"Umm . . . The mice have to get to the cheese shop before it closes." It was nice to know I could think quickly when I was almost up to my ears in mice. "Let them go. Okay?"

"Okay." She opened the front door. "Shoo. Go away," she said. Then she went to her room. I guess all that marching had tired her out. The mice ran outside and scattered in all directions.

But they had left behind a terrible mouse mess.

That's when Mom walked in. "Ed, what happened to the floor?" she asked.

"I . . . Libby . . . the mice . . ." Unlike Derwin, I had a lot fewer than a thousand words, and none of them seemed to fit together. I sighed and said, "I'll get the broom."

It took so long to sweep the floor clean that I was late for the party. Mom had already dropped Derwin off there. I grabbed my bathing suit and hurried out.

I was half a block from home when I heard someone behind me call, "Hi, Ed!"

It was my friend Quentin One. I had three friends named Quentin, so I called them Quentin One, Quentin Two, and Quentin Three.

Quentin One

"Are you going to the party?" I asked.

"Sure. Want a ride?" Quentin asked as he coasted past me on his bike.

"No thanks." The last time we'd tried that, we'd crashed.

"I'll see you there," he said, giving me a wave.

I was about to wave back. Then I realized that, even though Quentin was pedaling away, somehow he was still facing me. I hadn't seen him turn around.

"What in the world . . . ?"

I thought about all the strange things that had happened since I'd found the coin. *Could all this strangeness be connected to it?*

By the time I reached the hotel, I knew what I had to do. I pulled the coin from my pocket and flipped it into the bushes. Then I went inside, hoping things would be back to normal.

SHAKING UP IS HARD TO DO

Moose is the biggest kid in our class. He's also the smartest kid I know. He always finds unusual ways to solve problems.

The party was nicely normal at first. We swam, splashed, and ate snacks.

Moose

After a while, Quentin One climbed out of the pool. He headed for the locker room.

Just then, Quentin Two came in, hopping toward the pool on his pogo stick. He looked a lot like Quentin One. I guess he also looked like Quentin Three. I'd never noticed that before.

Quentin Two hopped over to me and said, "Hey, I saw you drop this. I'll bet you're glad you didn't lose it." He stopped hopping and held out the coin.

"Thanks." I was afraid to take it. But I was more afraid not to take it. I put it in the pocket of my bathing suit.

Moose and I sat by the side of the pool, drinking cherry cola. Most of the kids had brought blow-up rafts or float tubes. They were bobbing on the water like a bunch of Halloween apples.

"I wish we had rafts," I told Moose.

"It would be nice," he said.

"It's *your* birthday," I said. "I'm sure someone would let you borrow a raft."

"But then they wouldn't have one," Moose said. "There has to be a better answer."

Just then, Derwin walked past us, draining the last of his soda. He let out a loud burp.

"I got it! What a great idea!" Moose leaped up and grabbed Derwin. "Drink this," he said, handing his soda to my brother.

Derwin slugged the soda right down: **Gulp!**
Gulp! Gulp!

"Give him yours," Moose said.

"I'm still thirsty," I said.

"Just give it to him," Moose told me. "Quick, before he burps again."

"Yeah," Derwin said. "Just give it to me."

I handed over my soda. I didn't know what the rush was, but I really couldn't turn Moose down on his birthday.

Derwin gulped my soda so fast, it was like seeing bathwater vanish down the drain of a tub.

Moose clamped a hand over Derwin's mouth. Then he grabbed the back of his bathing suit. He lifted him up and started shaking him like he was one of those cool rattly things they use to make music in Mexican bands. Maracas — that's it. Shake, shake, shake.

MARACAS

"Whatever you do, keep your mouth closed," Moose said as he gave Derwin a final shake.

Derwin's mouth was shut tight. He started to swell with gas. He held his breath as Moose tossed him in the pool. Then Moose jumped onto Derwin. My brother bobbed a bit, but he had enough gas in his stomach to keep floating.

It worked great.
Until Derwin burped, that is.

The moment he opened his mouth, he shot
out from under Moose like a flyaway balloon.

He made it halfway across the bottom of the pool before he ran out of gas.

"Are you all right?" I asked when Derwin popped to the surface.

"Sure. That was fun," he said as he climbed out of the pool. "Let's do it again."

Moose tapped me on the shoulder. "Your turn to float," he said. But I couldn't stay. "Can you walk Derwin home?" I asked Moose. "Sure," he said.

I left the hotel. I needed to find out why everything became so strange the moment I found that coin. And I knew the perfect place to get some answers. . . .

CURIOUS ANSWERS

"Can I help you?" Mr. Sage asked when I walked into the New Curiosity Shop.

"I hope so." I pulled the coin from my pocket and handed it to him. "Can you tell me anything about this?"

"The Silver Center? I've heard stories about this coin, but I never believed the coin was real," he said. "Oh, dear. Was it this faded when you found it?" He held the coin up for me to see.

"No," I said. "It looked brand-new." The face of the coin reminded me of the really worn Buffalo nickel that my uncle gave me last year. I added "fading coin" to my list of strange experiences.

"There isn't much time," he said. "You need to give this coin to the Stranger."

"I'm not allowed to talk to strangers," I said.

"Not that kind of stranger," Mr. Sage said. "This is a special meaning of Stranger. If you don't give this to the Stranger before the words fade away, the world will lose all its strangeness."

"That doesn't sound like a bad thing," I said. *If there was no strangeness, I'd be more like everyone else.* I liked that idea.

"It would be terrible," he said. "Think of all the great people who seem strange. Remember the brilliant scientist Albert Einstein? And the amazing artist Pablo Picasso?

Einstein

Picasso

"They were both quite strange. Our greatest artworks and inventions happened because someone had a strange idea or saw a strange sight. Without strangeness, the world would be terribly dull."

"But things are *really* strange right now," I said. "Too strange."

"That should start to settle down once you give the Stranger the coin," Mr. Sage said.

"Maybe *you* should find this Stranger," I said.

He handed the coin back to me. "No. You found the coin. Or the coin found you. Either way, the job is yours."

"But I still don't know what to do," I said.

"Let your experiences guide you," Mr. Sage said. "A task this important would never fall into the hands of someone who couldn't handle it."

"I hope you're right," I said. I headed out.

This was awful. I hadn't learned a thing. And I sure didn't agree with him that strangeness was important. On top of that, he'd given me a job I didn't know how to do.

Wait!

I didn't need to know who I was looking for! If I gave the coin to every person I met, one of them would have to be the Stranger.

Mr. Sage didn't say I'd only get one chance. As soon as I got home, I handed the coin to Derwin. "Can you hold on to this for me?"

"Sure," he said. "Hey, Moose said we should go over and see all his presents."

"We?" I asked.

"Of course! You know everything's more fun when I'm around," Derwin said.

"I guess you can come." He could be a pest at times, but he was kind of fun.

We headed toward Moose's house. We were almost there when Derwin screamed, "Ouch! It's hot." He pointed at his pocket. "Help! Take it back!"

chapter 8

NEED A LIFT?

I pulled the coin from Derwin's pocket. It felt cold.

"Was that a trick coin?" he asked.

"I'm afraid so," I said as I put it back in my pocket.

When we got to Moose's house, his older brother, Mouse, answered the door.

Everyone calls him "Mouse" because he's nowhere near as big as Moose. Mouse doesn't come up with wild ideas like Moose, but he's stronger than Moose and he loves to talk.

There was a huge package on Moose's front porch.

"Moose," Mouse called, "you got something."

Moose came to the porch. "Oofff!" he said as he lifted the package.

Derwin looked at Moose and said, "I wish I was as strong as you."

"What about me?" Mouse said. "I'm stronger than Moose. I can lift anything." He grabbed Moose by the legs and lifted both him and the package straight up.

"I'll bet you can't lift *yourself*," I said.

"Sure I can," Mouse said. He put his brother down, squatted, and jammed his hands behind his knees.

"Stop!" I said. "I was joking."

"Oofff!" Mouse grunted as he lifted.

"Wow." That was about all I could say as I watched Mouse lift himself up in the air.

"Let go," I told him.

"I can't," Mouse said. "If I let go, I'll fall and get hurt."

He was five feet up, and still rising.

Moose rushed under his brother and held out his arms. "Just let go," he said. "We'll catch you."

Mouse shook his head.

I leaped up and tried to grab Mouse's feet, but he was too high.

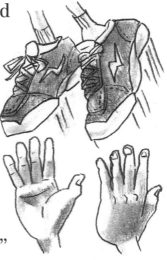

"I know," Derwin said. He ran to the garage, and came back with a piece of rope. "Catch!" he called to Mouse as he threw one end of the rope up in the air.

Mouse caught the rope with his teeth. Derwin, holding on to the other end, started to rise. Mouse was now lifting both of them into the air.

"Help me!" Derwin shouted.

Moose and I grabbed the rope right above Derwin's hands and started pulling. It was a real battle, but between us, we managed to get Derwin all the way down, and Mouse close to the ground.

"Thanks," Mouse said.

This was one time when good manners were a bad idea. When Mouse spoke, the rope fell out of his mouth. I guess that startled him, because he lifted himself even harder and shot right back up.

Derwin threw him the rope again, and Mouse chomped his teeth on it just like he did before. We all pulled. When Mouse was almost down, I warned him, "Don't say anything this time."

"I won't," he said.

Out came the rope. Up went Mouse.

We tried again. This time, I looked at Moose, and Moose looked at Derwin, and Derwin looked at me. Then we all looked up at Mouse and shouted, "Don't open your mouth, Moose!"

That worked. We got him back down. Once his feet were on the ground, he finally stopped lifting. Mouse wasn't as smart as Moose, but he did learn things sooner or later.

Moose opened the heavy package. It was a set of barbells.

I didn't stay long. I had too much to think about. As I walked home, I touched the coin. I still didn't know who to give it to. And I didn't like the idea that Mouse and Derwin could have gotten hurt today. Strangeness could be dangerous.

I checked the coin again right before bed. The words were almost totally faded. If I wanted to let the world lose all its strangeness, I wouldn't have long to wait. But if I was going to find the Stranger, I had to do it soon.

chapter 9

DIG DOG

A strange sound woke me Sunday morning.

I looked across at my five goldfish. Each

one swam to the bottom, picked up a piece of gravel in its mouth, and spat it out — hard — at the glass sides of the bowl.

PING! PING!

PING!

PING!

PING!

It looked like they were trying to break free.

When I have a tough problem to solve, I like to sit under the old apple tree in the backyard and think. So I headed out back.

Rex and Willow were there. I watched Rex dig a hole. When he was finished, he used his teeth to grab Willow by the scruff of the neck. I expected her to hiss and scratch. But she purred so loudly, I could hear her from halfway across the yard.

Rex dropped Willow in the hole.

"What are you doing?" I asked.

He ignored me, turned around, and kicked the dirt back in.

"Stop that!"

Rex sat at the edge of the hole. He was panting with that dog expression that looks kind of like a smile and also kind of like he has a stomachache.

I rushed over to rescue Willow. But Rex began to dig again. A moment later, Willow leaped out of the hole and started to lick herself clean.

Great. Most cats get hair balls. My cat is going to cough up mud balls.

Rex walked to a different part of the yard and started to dig another hole. Willow followed him. So did I.

I couldn't stand all the strangeness. I had to do something.

Anyone who's ever been on a merry-go-round knows how slowly it turns when you stand at the center. The farther out you go, the faster things spin. My brother, my sisters, my pets, and my friends were standing far from the center, way out in the Looniverse. They'd always been strange, but now it was like they were clinging to the very edge, with their feet flying in the air. I was in the center, the only normal person of us all.

After Rex finished digging, I waited until he picked up Willow. Then I tossed the coin into the hole.

Rex instantly dropped Willow.

"Good boy," I said.

Rex started to fill the hole. I went to check my fish. They were swimming around like normal. Burying the coin seemed to have worked.

Just to be safe, I went out back to make sure the coin was still buried.

When I got there, I found Sarah Beth, Derwin, Libby, Quentin One, Moose, and Mouse all there. They stopped talking the instant they saw me.

Now I really felt left out. "What's going on?" I asked.

"We want to talk to you," Sarah Beth said.

"Right now," Moose added.

I felt a ripple in my stomach. I'd never seen them look so serious.

chapter 10

STRANGE TRUTHS

"What do you want to talk about?" I asked.

They stood there, looking at one another, and at the ground, and at the clouds — but not at me. *What could be so terrible that they were afraid to tell me?* I wondered.

Finally, Derwin stood on his tiptoes and whispered something to Moose. Then Moose stepped forward.

"Well," he said, "we wish you'd try to be a little less strange."

"Me?" I asked. I couldn't have been more surprised if he had told me there was a kangaroo on my head.

"You," Moose said.

"What are you guys talking about?" I asked. "There's nothing strange about me. Right now, I'm the *only* normal person around here."

"No way," Moose said. "Strange stuff happens when you're around."

"It sure does," Libby said. "After you read that story to me, all those mice showed up."

Mouse nodded. "I got stuck in the air when you came over."

"I got the strangest twisty feeling when I rode my bike past you," Quentin One said.

"You're the one who told me about the thousand words," Derwin said. "My hand *still* hurts!"

"I only have trouble with my food when you're at dinner," Sarah Beth said.

"Things have always been a little strange around you," Moose said. "But they seem to be getting even stranger lately."

"Definitely stranger," Sarah Beth said.

"Stranger for sure," Derwin said. I felt like I'd been punched in the stomach. How could they blame *me* for the way *they* had been acting? "This isn't fair," I said. "And I don't like the way you're ganging up on me."

"Look," Derwin said, "all we're asking is that you try to be a little more normal."

"Think about it," Moose said.

I watched, shocked and hurt, as all the two-legged creatures left the backyard. I went up to my room, alone, and thought about everything.

If I did nothing, and let the coin fade without giving it to the Stranger, I would remove all strangeness from the world.

Was that what I wanted?

I thought about how both
Derwin and Moose had
shouted, "What a great
idea!" I thought about all the
wonderful paintings, movies, and
books that must have started out
as strange ideas. Did I
want a world without any
strangeness?

No!

I ran out back, grabbed
a shovel, and dug up the coin.

When I saw it, my heart sank. The face was smooth and blank. I looked closer, but I could barely make out the "r" in "stranger." I needed to give the coin to the Stranger immediately. *But I still don't know who it is.*

"Think!" I told myself.

I remembered Mr. Sage's words. *Let your experiences guide you.*

I thought about my experiences since I'd found the coin. Derwin made a saying become real. Sarah Beth's train moved. Libby's mice showed up. Moose got a swell idea. Mouse lifted himself. My pets acted weird. Then everyone blamed me for their strangeness.

Their words echoed through my mind:

GETTING EVEN STRANGER LATELY

DEFINITELY STRANGER

STRANGER FOR SURE

It all fell together. I finally knew who the stranger was!

chapter 11

NORMALLY STRANGE?

I thought about Derwin's pencils. A sharpener makes things sharper. A sweetener makes things sweeter.

The Stranger makes things stranger!

"Could it be?" I whispered. *Am I the Stranger?*

But if I was the Stranger, why were the words fading?

I realized there was one more thing I had to do.

"You're mine," I whispered to the coin. The silver coin glowed like the moon. The words rose up, solid and bold. I watched the sky as the moon rose and fell.

This time, I knew it wasn't my imagination. And I knew that strangeness was no longer in danger of fading away. I smiled, knowing I'd made the right decision.

The sad part was that my friends and family wouldn't want me around anymore. I wasn't sure I'd be able to get used to that.

Far off, I heard an ice-cream truck. Maybe a strawberry ice pop would cheer me up. I went around to the front yard. Derwin, Moose, and the others were standing there, waiting for me. Quentin One was gone, but Quentin Three was there on his skateboard.

"We're sorry about what we said," Sarah Beth told me.

"It's pretty boring when you're not around," Moose said.

"Very boring," Derwin agreed. "Nothing fun happens."

"So you want me around again?" I asked.

"Absolutely," they all said.

"That's great!" I said. The music of the ice-cream truck moved closer.

"Buy me an ice cream," Libby said.

"MONEY DOESN'T GROW ON TREES," I told her.

"Maybe it grows under them," Derwin said.

"Let's see." Mouse lifted up an oak tree and looked under it.

"Hey, I found a dollar bill," said Derwin.

I felt a small tingle of excitement. My words had caused the strangeness. *Could I learn to control my strange new power?*

Derwin scooped up the dollar and held it out. When the ice-cream truck drove past  us, the driver handed Derwin a cone. He took the dollar without even stopping.

"Your cone looks like a rocket ship," Sarah Beth said.

She grabbed the ice-cream cone from Derwin and turned it upside down. It shot up into the air. I felt another tingle. I guess I'd helped make her imagination do strange things.

"I'll get it," Mouse said. He took off, running so fast his feet didn't touch the ground.

Quentin Three chased after him. The wheels fell off his skateboard, but he kept on going.

"Read me a story?" Libby asked.

"Sure," I told her. "Go pick a good one. No mice, this time. And no snakes or giant spiders, either. Okay?"

"Okay." She ran toward the house. Halfway there, she stopped and asked, "Dragons?"

"Only if they're small and friendly," I called back. I spotted Mr. Sage across the street. I held up the coin in one hand, and then pointed at myself with the other.

Mr. Sage nodded and smiled. Then he walked off. But I was sure I'd be seeing him again.

"I am the Stranger," I whispered to myself. I liked the way that sounded. I thought about how I'd had to give the coin to myself. I guess it made sense that the Stranger would have a strange start.

It felt good to be standing in the center of my very own Looniverse — with strange and amazing adventures ahead of me.

Check out
the next
LOONIVERSE book!

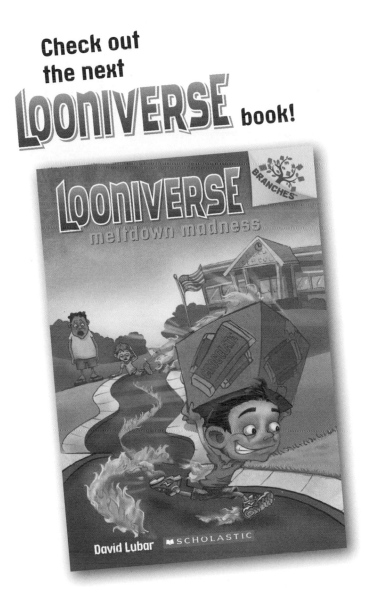

DAVID LUBAR is no stranger to strangeness, having written all sorts of weirdly funny books such as *Beware the Ninja Weenies and Other Warped and Creepy Tales*. He has a girl cat with a boy's name, a left-handed guitar, and a small collection of plush arachnids. He sometimes uses a big word like "arachnid" when a small word like "spider" would work just fine, but he's basically a nice guy otherwise. Though he grew up in Morristown, NJ, and now lives in Nazareth, PA, he makes frequent visits to the Looniverse to snatch ideas from Ed and the gang.

MATT LOVERIDGE and strange are old friends — they go way back. Right from birth there have been strange coincidences in his life. When he was born he weighed 13 pounds, he wears size 13 shoes, and to top it all off he's 13 feet tall. Okay, maybe he's not 13 feet tall, but he is the tallest little brother in his family. Now that he's all grown up, he likes hiking, biking, and drinking milk from the carton. He lives in the mountains of Utah with his wife and kids, and their black dog named Blue.